PEPPERMINT MURDER

The Frosted Love Cozy Mystery Series,
Book 22

SUMMER PRESCOTT

Summer Prescott Books Publishing

Cupcakes in Paradise owner, Melissa Gladstone-Beckett added the last twirly dollop of red and white striped peppermint icing with a flourish. Missy had baked her luscious Double-Chocolate cupcakes and topped them with the latest recipe that she'd invented for fluffy Peppermint Icing, adding a tiny candy cane on top of each one to make them extra festive. The petite blonde loved the holidays more than just about anything, and had been delighted to create new and exciting cupcake and frosting flavors.

She had half a dozen guests coming to stay at the Beach House Inn, which she and her husband,

Detective Chas Beckett owned, and had been commissioned to provide a holiday party for the group. The inn and cupcake shop were located right next door to each other on Florida's Gulf Coast, in the tiny town of Calgon. Missy had coffee every morning at *Cupcakes in Paradise*, with her best friend, Echo Willis, a laid-back former Californian, and Phillip "Kel" Kellerman, the town gossip and incredibly talented artist who owned the gallery at which Echo worked. Kel felt that it was part of his civic duty to bring newcomers Missy and Echo up to speed on all of the latest happenings in Calgon, and was a faithful fan of Missy's cupcakes.

"Hey, girlfriend," Echo called out as she came into the kitchen. "Ohhhh...those look amazing," the redhead breathed, gazing hungrily at the cupcakes. "Any vegan ones?" she asked hopefully. Missy almost always concocted a vegan version of her new recipes so that Echo, and any other vegans who happened to come along, would be able to enjoy the treats. Some folks in town ate them just because they assumed that "vegan" meant "healthy."

"Of course," Missy grinned. "Take one from the tray over there. The ones with the green sprinkles are vegan," she pointed in the general direction of the vegan tray of cupcakes with her frosting bag. "Grab a carnivorous one for Kel while you're at it," she directed, squeezing the leftover frosting into a container.

"You got it. I already put fresh coffee on out front, so once you're done here, we can get down to the serious business of catching up on what's been happening in our fair town," Echo replied, plating the cupcakes for the three of them and heading for their favorite bistro table in the front of the shop.

Missy put a lid on the container of frosting, peeled her work gloves off, tossing them in the trash, and put the tips in a mesh bag for the dishwasher. She took a chair across from Kel, who was seated and reading his paper awaiting fresh coffee and cupcakes.

"Good morning, lovely lady," he greeted her with a smile.

"Hey, Kel. I hope you like peppermint," Missy said, glancing at the cupcake in front of him.

"Dear Missy, there are very few culinary delights that I don't like," he reminded her, peeling the festive pleated cup from his cupcake and taking a huge bite to illustrate his point.

"So, what's new in town?" Echo asked, settling in at the table.

"Well, ever since your boy, Spencer, and I went to The Marvelous Mail shipping store last week, I'm afraid Dora Hartshorn, who works there, has seen fit to send me some rather scandalous emails," he confided, shaking his head in disbelief. Echo cracked up and Missy's eyes widened. Spencer was a young handsome Marine veteran who worked at the inn as a handyman, server and general go-to guy. He'd gone along with Kel when the artist was fishing for information from the brassy, fifty-something, Dora.

"Is that why I heard you gasp in the office yesterday afternoon?" Echo, his Gallery Manager, teased.

"Indeed," he shuddered. "I'm not necessarily one who conforms to the bounds of societal propriety, but that woman appears to have some rather disturbing issues."

"You're just irresistible, Kel," it was Missy's turn for some good-natured ribbing.

"So it would seem," the artist replied with a grimace. "Has my lovely Gallery Manager informed you that I'm hosting a gala next week that I would like you and your hubby to attend?"

"Yes, she did, and I will gladly use your event as an excuse to buy a new dress," she beamed.

"Perfect. Is it too late to place an order for goodies for the event?" Kel looked at her hopefully.

"Not at all," Missy patted his hand. "Just decide what you need and have your GM fax me an order."

"I emailed it to you this morning," Echo said, sipping her coffee.

"What would I do without her?" the artist looked at his employee with more than admiration.

"Starve your guests for one thing," she replied lightly. "So, what else is happening out there in the wild world of Calgon?"

"Sadly, I have little else to report. It seems that no one breaks up, gets divorced or sues their family during the holidays. Good will to all men and that sort of thing, you know," he shrugged sadly.

"Well, here's to hoping for a lascivious New Year," Missy joked, raising her coffee mug for a toast.

"Here, here," Kel replied, clinking his mug against hers while Echo polished off her vegan cupcake.

The bells above the door jangled, admitting Spencer Bengal.

"Hey, everybody," he raised a hand, greeting the group. "Mrs. Beckett, Maggie sent me over to let you know that your guests have arrived. She thought you might want to meet them," the strapping young Marine informed Missy.

"Definitely. Help yourself to some cupcakes, Spence," she gestured to the tray in the center of the table. "Is it a family?"

"No ma'am," he replied, reaching for a cupcake. "It's three couples. I'd say they're in their mid-40's or so."

"Oh, how fun! People our age," she nudged Echo. "You and Kel will have to come to afternoon tea and introduce yourselves. And I'm probably going to invite Carla, so you'll have to behave," she warned her flame-haired friend.

"Do you have to invite her?" Echo sighed. To say that she and Missy's interior decorator, Carla Mayhew, didn't get along, was more than a bit of an understatement. The two women were like oil and water.

"I'm trying to help her stay sober."

"By inviting her to an event where there's plenty of free wine and beer?" Echo raised an eyebrow.

"Just be nice. Please? I'm going to make sure that she talks to people and has a good time without getting drunk," Missy gave her bestie a pointed look.

"As long as she realizes that I'm not on the menu," Kel tried to lighten the mood with a joke.

"I have every confidence that you'll be able to take care of yourself, Kel."

"If I don't, no one else will," he grumbled with a smile.

"Spencer, can you take care of the shop while I go meet the new guests?" Missy asked.

"I'll guard it with my life, ma'am," the Marine grinned, his cheeks full of cupcake.

Chapter 2

*C*arla Mayhew made her way to the kitchen to make coffee, feeling weak and shaky. She had refused to take a drink of alcohol for the past three days, and her body felt as though it had been hit by a truck. Her head pounded, her throat was so dry that it ached, and she felt faint every time that she sat up, stood, or moved more than a few feet. She ignored the rolling of her stomach, having thrown up so many times in the past couple of days that she knew surely there could be nothing left to spew.

The interior decorator had spent most of the previous two days, either shaking and shuddering in the sweat-stained sheets of her bed, or hurling whatever water and sports drink that she had managed to force down into the toilet. She knew that Missy would have been on her doorstep in a heartbeat, with hugs and homemade soup, but she was ashamed of the state that she was in, and was determined to tough it out on her own, even if it killed her. She'd cried out several times in the past few days, thinking that death would actually be a welcome respite.

Today, despite the dizziness and queasiness that she'd come to expect, Carla was beginning to feel a tiny bit better. Beneath the nausea, she felt the beginning pangs of hunger, and her craving for coffee was profound enough to drive her from her bed in order to make it. She wished that there was a local shop that would deliver coffee and doughnuts, but such was not the case, so she headed to the kitchen in her fluffy blue chenille robe, pale and weary, but feeling the slightest ray of hope.

Realizing that she'd been detached from the real world long enough, Carla made the coffee, and while it was brewing, decided to go to the box at the end of her driveway to collect three days worth of newspapers. First, she took a long, slow drink of ice cold water, feeling the chill of it hit the bottom of her stomach. Refreshed, she tied the sash of her robe around her snugly, and headed for the front door. Just inside her foyer, she slipped her feet into the black flip flops that she used to go to the paper box and mail box, opening the door and seeing the sunlight for the first time in days.

Carla's 1950's ranch home was near the crest of a small hill, and her driveway sloped downward from the street to the front door that was tucked back into a courtyard. She trudged slowly up the drive, and when she got to the top, leaned shakily on the pole which supported the mail and paper boxes. A movement out of the corner of her eye caught her attention, and what she saw made her think that perhaps she was hallucinating. Rubbing her eyes and blinking rapidly, she realized that, either her hallucination wasn't going away, or it wasn't a hallucination at all, which was a horrific proposition.

The tiny girl had long, unkempt blonde hair, and

was dressed in a pink nightgown, the hem of which was drenched in blood. Her feet were bare, and her big blue eyes were wide and unblinking, seeming to have no life in them at all. She was carrying a small, well-loved brown bear in one arm, and the fingers of her other hand were in her mouth. There were blood stains on her hands, face and nightie, and for a moment, Carla stood stock still, too shocked to even speak.

"Hey, there," Carla called softly, as the little girl padded slowly down the middle of the street. It was evident that the poor little waif clearly needed some help, and she didn't want to scare her, so she walked toward her slowly. The girl stopped, and her head turned almost mechanically when she heard the voice calling out to her. Staring at Carla, she stood rooted to her spot.

"Are you okay, honey?" the decorator asked, crouching down so that she was on the same level. The girl blinked twice.

"Mommy hurt," she said somberly, briefly taking her fingers out of her mouth.

"Your Mommy is hurt?" Carla confirmed, reaching out to touch the toddler's shoulder.

The cherub-faced tot nodded.

"Okay. I'm going to help you, sweetie," she said, reaching for the girl's hand. "Let's go into my house. I'll get you a cookie and call a nice policeman to come over and help your mama, okay?"

The girl nodded again and placed her saliva-soaked hand into Carla's.

Chapter 3

"Sweetheart, I'm going to want you to come with me on this one," Chas told Missy gravely, as he hit the button to end his call with Carla. "Just until the DCFS rep arrives. I'll explain in the car on the way over. I'm going to call an ambulance and some backup, and then we'll be leaving."

"Oh, my. Okay. I'll give Echo a call and ask her to open up the shop without me this morning," she said, reaching for her cell.

Adrenaline had coursed through Missy's body when her husband asked her to come along, and when she heard why, she was even more concerned.

"I hate to ask, but..." she couldn't bring herself to finish her sentence.

"Do I think Carla is involved?" Chas seemed to read her mind, as usual. "I doubt it. With a situation like this, most people would run fast and far if they were involved. Carla is your friend...do you know of any conflicts that she may have had with her neighbors?"

Missy shook her head. "No, but then, when she's drinking, you never know who she might have a conflict with," she sighed.

"Well, I guess we'll find out soon enough," the detective gripped the steering wheel a bit tighter.

When they arrived, the little blonde-haired girl was sitting on a chair at the kitchen table, nibbling on a chocolate chip cookie, and Carla was drinking coffee as though she were drawing strength from the dark brew. Missy's heart went out to the quiet, grubby-but-beautiful little girl, and, after giving Carla a hug, she went and knelt in front of her.

"Hi," she smiled at the child. "I'm Missy. What's your name?"

The girl said something with a mouthful of cookie that was unintelligible to everyone but Missy.

"Your name is Emi?" she asked, just to make sure, and the child nodded, drawing surprised looks from Carla and Chas as the decorator brought the detective up to speed in a low voice.

"That's such a pretty name. Is this your bear?" she asked, patting the disheveled stuffed animal on Carla's table. Another nod.

"He's really cute. What's his name?"

"Sam." The child licked some melted chocolate from between her fingers, and regarded Missy curiously. "Nuther cookie?" she asked.

"Of course you can have another cookie," Missy said, reaching for the cellophane sleeve of cookies on the counter top. "Here you go. Did you have breakfast this morning, sweetie?"

Emi shook her head no.

"What about dinner? Did you have dinner last night?"

"Yup," she chewed, her attention entirely on the cookie. She saw Missy staring at her hands, and looked down at them herself. "Dirty," she said, holding the one without the cookie out in front of her.

A glance passed between Missy and Chas.

"I know, sweetie, but very soon, a nice police officer is going to come and help you clean up, okay?"

Missy knew that the forensics team would want to take samples of the blood from Emi's hands, face, feet and nightgown, so she tried to make it sound like a positive thing, hoping that the little girl wouldn't be scared when the time came. Emi nodded and returned her focus back to the cookie. Chas called Missy over for a moment and gave her some instructions. She returned to the little girl and knelt down in front of her again.

"Emi, if we go outside, can you show me where your house is?"

"Yup," the toddler said, not looking up from her cookie.

An additional police car and an ambulance arrived at Carla's and needed direction to the possible crime scene.

"Do you want to ride in a police car?" Missy asked, trying to make it sound fun and exciting, knowing that the officers in the cruiser would be keeping the child safe.

"Kay," Emi replied, climbing down from the chair and putting her tiny hand in Missy's.

They rode down the street, in the direction from which she had come. Once it was time to transport the child, a representative of the child welfare office would bring a car seat, but for now, time was of the essence, so they had to make do. Sitting, buckled in securely, on Missy's lap in the backseat, as Chas drove very slowly, flashers on, Emi identified her house, a nicely-kept ranch that was pretty typical for the upper middle-class neighborhood.

"Go home?" she asked, her blue eyes wide with innocence. Missy's heart broke.

"Not right now, sweetie. We're going to go back to Miss Carla's house and get you all cleaned up, okay?"

The child's lower lip started to pooch out just a bit.

"And we'll have some breakfast," Missy added quickly.

"Kay," Emi said sadly, her head turning to look at her house as the cruiser turned around to drop them off at Carla's.

When they went back into the kitchen, Carla had risen to the occasion and was already preparing breakfast. The DCFS representative had arrived, along with a member of the forensics team who, thankfully, was a father of four little ones himself, and knew just how to keep little Emi entertained while he swabbed samples from her skin and clothing. Chas had followed the ambulance and other patrol cars over to the house that Emi had said was hers. The officers knew that they were on the right track when they saw tiny little bloody footprints coming down the sidewalk from a front door that was left ajar. After taking in the scene, Chas made a quick call to the social worker. Emi wouldn't be going home tonight.

Chapter 4

"Poor little lamb," Echo clucked, her heart breaking for the traumatized child.

"What were the parent's names?" Kel asked, leaning forward with a frown.

"Melany and Garret Anderson, but they weren't the only ones who were murdered," Missy replied sadly. "There was another woman at the house..."

"Let me guess, Marcia Stanton?" the artist supplied.

Missy stared at him in astonishment. "Yes. How did you know that?"

"The two have been best friends their entire lives, it wasn't much of a challenge."

"But why on earth would someone randomly kill everyone in the house except for a young child?" Echo wondered.

"The social worker said that Emi hid in a kitchen cabinet when she heard unfamiliar noises and adults yelling. She came out after the noise stopped, and not knowing what to do, she went to her bed to hide, eventually falling asleep. She woke up yesterday morning and wandered out of the house in shock."

"Nothing like this has ever happened in Calgon," Kel shook his head. "Does Chas have any leads?"

"He hasn't said anything about it, other than to say that there was no sign of forced entry, so whoever it was, most likely had some sort of connection to the family."

"That's pretty typical," the artist replied. "Murders tend to be personal, rather than random."

"Did you know the Andersons?" Missy asked.

"Not personally. I knew of them because Melany's parents were art collectors. Garret worked for the local TV news station as a reporter. The friend, Marcia Stanton married well and attended every social and charitable event in town. We worked on the Annual Art Fair together a few times. I have some suspicions that I'm going to check out," Kel set his mug down, nodding to himself.

"You think you might know who did it?" Echo asked, her brows arched in surprise.

"Possibly. I'm going to try to sniff some things out."

"Well, keep us posted, so that I can let Chas know what you're up to," Missy directed.

"In good time, my dear."

Carla's arrival at the cupcake shop was heralded by the bells at the door.

"Hey, all," she said, looking better than they had seen her looking in months.

"Hey, girl. How are you holding up after all the excitement yesterday?" Missy asked.

The decorator shrugged. "I can't get the image of that precious little girl, looking so lost and alone, out of my mind."

"I'm so glad that you were there to take her in. Who knows what might have happened if you hadn't seen her."

"I just wish I could've done more. I'm just thankful that kids are so resilient. Hopefully she'll never remember any of this," Carla shook her head. "She left her bear at my house," she held out a shopping bag to Missy. "Can you make sure that it gets to her?"

"Of course." Missy took the bag and tucked it away under the front counter.

"Marcia Stanton was a client of yours, wasn't she?" Kel asked.

Carla looked at him quizzically. "Yes, why?" When all three were silent, she looked from one to another, realization finally dawning on her. "Oh my...was she...?"

Missy nodded sadly.

"Good criminy," the decorator paled, sighing heavily. "Why the heck does all of this have to happen when I'm busy trying to get sober? If there was ever a time that I could use a good, stiff shot..." she muttered.

"I know of some herbal remedies that might help," Echo offered quietly. She and Carla had nearly no charitable feelings toward one another, but the fiery champion of all things good had nothing but respect for the decorator's efforts. "I think it takes a lot of strength to do what you're doing."

"Thanks, I might take you up on that," was the simple response.

Kel and Missy exchanged a quick glance, both were amazed at the first civilized exchange that Carla and Echo had ever shared.

"Hey, since you're here, do you mind if I pick your brain a bit? I have a holiday party happening this weekend, and I could use some help with the extra decorating, if you have time," Missy asked Carla, wanting to get her more involved in positive endeavors.

"That sounds just like what the doctor ordered," the decorator nodded. "Would you happen to have a Salted Caramel cupcake for me to munch on the way? I'm starving."

"Well, that's a good sign, and yes, as a matter of fact I do," Missy smiled, going to fetch the treat.

Kel looked at Echo after the two of them left. "Do I see a shred of compassion in your soul for Miss Carla?" he teased.

"You know me...champion of the underdog...even if she's catty," Echo stood and started clearing the dishes. "What's on your agenda this morning?" she deftly changed the subject.

"I'm going to start exploring a few of my ideas about whodunit before I head to the gallery. I'm assuming that you're holding the fort down here while Missy keeps Carla busy?"

Echo nodded, heading for the kitchen. "Those cupcakes won't frost themselves."

Chapter 5

*B*etsy's Diner was a gathering place for locals that was famous for its abundant breakfasts and heavenly slabs of pie. The décor hadn't changed since the seventies, and that was just the way that the townsfolk liked it. Betsy Boggus, the owner and sole proprietor was a reliable source of gossip, particularly since she typically saw townspeople when they came in bright-eyed and loud after a night on the town, or bedraggled and sleepy the next morning. Her place was open 24/7 except for Christmas day, and on other holidays, she often fed those who needed it for free.

"Well, Phillip Kellerman, as I live and breathe," Betsy rasped when Kel took his seat at the counter.

There were patrons at a couple of booths in the back, but otherwise the diner was empty, giving the artist an ample opportunity to pick the owner's brain. "The usual, Sunshine?"

"Yes, please, my lovely," Kel grinned, looking forward to his buttermilk pancakes, eggs over-medium, bacon, sausage and home fries. The only downside to eating at Betsy's was that the woman could not make decent coffee to save her life. The food was spectacular in every cholesterol-filled, fat-inducing way, but to accompany it, he always ordered Earl Grey.

"Don't think that I don't know why you're here," Betsy accused good-naturedly, setting down several plates in from of him.

"Witty conversation and sublime breakfast?" the artist waggled his eyebrows playfully.

"Mmhmm..." the iron-haired gal made a face. "I heard about what happened to the Andersons and the Stanton woman, so I know that you heard about it too."

"It may have been mentioned."

Wiping down the counter in front of him and speaking softly enough that none of the other patrons could hear, Betsy asked him what he knew.

"Nothing, really. No details." Kel popped a bite of syrup drenched pancake in his mouth while she picked up a tray filled with clean glasses and began stacking them behind the counter nearby.

"My dishwasher, Leroy, moonlights over at Sam's Grille in Mescola," she said in a low voice, referring to a town in the middle of nowhere, about 45 minutes away from Calgon. "He works the midnight to six a.m. shift, and said that Melany was a frequent flyer out there," Betsy raised her eyebrows.

"A youngish wife and mother, spending her time at a dive in the boonies? That doesn't make much sense," Kel frowned, taking a bite of crisp bacon.

"It does if you take into account the company that she was keeping."

"Do tell..."

"A Mr. Calvin Cramer," Betsy raised her eyebrows knowingly.

"But...wasn't he married to...?"

"Her bestie, Marcia Stanton? Yes, he was," she nodded, pursing her lips.

"And they had a relationship of some sort?" the artist said delicately.

"Yes, they did. At least, it appeared that way to Leroy."

"Was it a murder/suicide then?" Kel asked, astonished.

"Not from what I heard. One of my waitresses dates a forensics guy, and from what I understand, everyone in the house, except for the poor little girl, was murdered in the same way, with the same weapon. One thing that I've always found a little bit interesting is the fact that both Melany and her husband have coal black hair and brown eyes, yet they managed to produce a beautiful little blonde, blue-eyed girl," Betsy looked at him pointedly.

"Just like Calvin Cramer," Kel actually put down his fork for a moment.

"You said it, not me," she raised her hands.

"I wonder if he has an alibi," the artist mused.

"I don't know, but if I was looking to find out, I'd check over at the Cambridge Club. I hear tell he spends a fair bit of time there," Betsy placed another pot of hot water and a fresh tea bag on a plate and set it in front of him.

"I'll have to dust off my membership, and enter that hallowed space that reeks of cigars and money," he replied wryly. Kel was more than successful, but pretentious people made him itch. "So, if Cal was spending time with Melany, who was keeping his lovely wife company, I wonder."

"Well, that's where it gets a bit complicated..."

"You don't mean..." the artist blinked. He wasn't a man who was easily shocked, but this particular morning had been full of surprises.

Betsy shrugged. "If the rumors are to be believed. Think about it, Kel. You've got a husband and wife who are stepping out, and a husband and wife who are left behind. Doesn't it make sense that they might turn to each other?"

"That's a whole lot of infidelity and subterfuge for just two families," the artist observed.

"Which could make for an explosive situation," she pointed out reasonably.

"Yes, but why would Cal kill his companion along with his wife and her companion?"

"Maybe he just wanted out of the whole mess. Who knows?" Betsy shrugged.

"Or, perhaps, there's something more powerful that motivated him."

"I'd be careful with this one, my friend," she warned. "Cal Cramer has lots of friends in high places. If he did do this, and finds out that you're on his trail, it could get dangerous." She cleared a mountain of empty plates while Kel dabbed at his mouth with a paper napkin.

"The greater they are, the harder they fall, dear woman," the artist replied with a gleam in his eye.

issy bustled about, emptying bags of sparkly fabric, blankets of cotton "snow", and boxes of icicles, ornaments and garlands for the "White Christmas" theme party that her guests had requested. They were a group of friends from a city a couple of hours away, who thought that it would be great fun to host their annual Christmas party at the stately B&B. No one would have to drive home, and other attendees had rented hotel rooms locally, so everyone would be safe. They were expecting around one hundred guests, which necessitated use of the ballroom, rather than one the parlors, and had hired a caterer for the drink and hors d'oeuvre service.

Carla was supposed to be there at any minute, and Missy was thankful to have her help with the decorations. Spencer had brought all of the bags and boxes in and was standing by to climb ladders, hammer nails and whatever else was needed for the decorating process. There were literally thousands of twinkle lights to be wrapped in cotton "snow" and suspended from the ceiling, doorways, pillars and around the windows that overlooked the beach. The patio area outside the ballroom's French doors would also be aglow with a central fire pit and more "snow" twinkle lights. While Missy was excited to see the ballroom decked out for the holidays, she was feeling the time crunch and her stress level was beginning to rise.

"You can stop frowning, I've come to save the day," Carla teased, coming up behind Missy as she punctured the plastic bag containing one of the faux snow blankets.

"Oh, my goodness, I'm so glad to see you," Missy exclaimed, giving the decorator a hug.

"Clearly," she chuckled, surveying the supplies and the undecorated room.

The two women, with Spencer's help, had decorated the rest of the inn, but had left the ballroom until last, knowing that the end result had to be magical. The massive mahogany fireplace in the center of the room would be the focal point, and the rest of the room would be turned into a wintry fairyland as well.

"Hey, muscles," Carla addressed the young Marine. "You ready to put your back into this?"

"Awaiting orders, ma'am," Spencer replied amiably.

The three of them worked for nearly four hours before taking a lunch break, and as they sat out on the patio, enjoying thick sandwiches made from last night's ham, Maggie came out with a worried look on her face.

"Missy...can I speak to you for a moment?" she asked.

"Of course." She put down her sandwich and followed the innkeeper back inside. "What's wrong?"

"Mr. Jeppson, the gentleman who made the reservation for the party, is thinking about canceling," Maggie told her in an urgent whisper.

"What? Why?" Missy's eyes widened in surprise.

"I'm not sure exactly, something about a death. He wants to speak with you. I had him wait in the Wedgewood Parlor."

"The food has been ordered, we just spent hours decorating, the DJ has been scheduled...if he cancels, it's going to be costly for him," Missy sighed, dreading the conversation that she was about to have with her guest. "Okay, Maggie. Thanks. I'll go talk to him."

Steve Jeppson was staring out the window, hands in pockets, when Missy entered the parlor.

"You wanted to see me, Mr. Jeppson?"

The handsome, sandy-haired guest turned from the window.

"Mrs. Beckett," he nodded a greeting. "Yes, I'm afraid I have some bad news. I just learned this morning that the wife of one of my invited guests has, tragically, been murdered. That whole sad state of affairs has put quite a pall on our enthusiasm for the event that we have scheduled, so I'm seriously considering canceling it."

Missy's heart went out to him. "How awful for you. I'm so sorry. Was it a close friend of yours?"

Steve shook his head. "No. A business associate from this area, Cal Cramer. I actually only met his wife, Marcia, once, briefly. Do you know him?"

Working very hard to not react at the mention of Cal Cramer's name, Missy kept her sympathetic expression firmly in place. "No, I'm afraid I don't. What an awful thing to deal with, particularly this close to the holidays."

"Agreed. Which is why I'm thinking of canceling the party."

Instead of approaching the situation with the realities of deposits that would need to be forfeited and inconveniences caused, Missy chose a different strategy.

"Don't you think that perhaps a gathering of people who care about and support him might be just the thing to ease his pain and help him see something positive in the midst of his grief?" she proposed.

Steve raised his eyebrows. "I hadn't actually considered that, but you may be right. Let me talk with the others and see what they think."

"And if you think that a huge, grand party might overwhelm him, you could always scale things back a bit and only invite those who actually know him," she suggested.

"That's not a bad idea," he nodded. "I'll see what the gang has to say and get back with you in a bit, if that's okay."

"Of course, take your time."

Chapter 7

Kel straightened his bow tie after handing off his keys to the valet at the Cambridge Club, convinced that he looked dapper enough to rub elbows with the elitist masters of the universe who spent their evenings sipping scotch, smoking cigars and making multi-million-dollar deals inside the mahogany-clad walls of the revered establishment. It had been a very long time since he'd graced these hallowed halls with his presence, but tonight, he was a man on a mission, and if he had to grossly overpay for a filet mignon accompanied by fine imported wine to accomplish his goal, so be it.

"Mr. Kellerman, welcome. It's lovely to see you

again," Francois, the concierge, greeted him like an old friend. Kel was one of the few club members who treated the Frenchman like a person rather than a servant, and because of that, he always received the best of service in return.

"Francois, it is always a pleasure," he shook the concierge's hand.

"Feel free to take any table that you'd like in the lounge. I'll have a server bring you a menu and a cocktail once you're seated."

"Thank you," Kel nodded at the man, and slipped him a fifty-dollar bill, just because he was glad to see a friendly face in a room full of magnates who passed judgment upon him for making a living as a "lowly" artist. The fact that his work was world renowned impressed few people in this particular venue.

He heard the creak of fine leather, as bottoms covered by five-thousand-dollar suits shifted in their chairs. Ice tinkled in glasses of scotch that cost nearly as much as most folks' monthly grocery bills, and thin smoke from Cuba's finest drifted lazily upward, getting smoothly sucked into the room's silent central vac system. A few members looked up curiously at the artist's arrival, then went back to their conversations with no acknowledgement of his presence, most ignored him entirely, not bothering to even glance in his direction, and a couple of gents who were avid collectors of his work nodded politely.

As predicted by Betsy, Cal Cramer was there, holding court at a table with two other gentlemen. By all outward appearances, he seemed perfectly content, sipping on a Manhattan and deeply engrossed in conversation. Kel couldn't get a table close enough to him to be able to listen in on the conversation, but he did find one that gave him a discreet sightline through the fronds of a potted palm, so that he could observe the "grieving" widower.

Francois was true to his word, as always, and as soon as Kel was seated, he was presented with a refreshing vodka tonic and a menu with no prices. If you were a member here, price wasn't an issue and one knew better than to ask. The server took his surf and turf order, and brought out his goose liver pate appetizer almost immediately. He had no idea how long Cal Cramer and friends would be in the Club, so he was preparing for a marathon evening. By all outward appearances, the artist was merely scrolling through the news feed on his phone and enjoying a mellow evening at the Cambridge. In reality, he was watching Cal Cramer like a hawk, hoping to glean whatever knowledge he could from his less-than-ideal location.

Kel was halfway through his succulent lobster tail and melt-in-your-mouth filet when Francois approached Cal and discreetly handed him a slip of folded paper. Opening the message, Cal scanned it quickly, raised his eyebrows briefly, and curiously, held it up to his nose for a moment before tucking it into the inside pocket of his Italian blazer. Taking the last swallow of yet another Manhattan, he shook hands with each of the two gentlemen at the table and made his way to the foyer.

Kel was torn. On the one hand, he wanted to try to follow the young mogul to see where he went and what he was doing. On the other hand, he was in the midst of the most delectable meal he'd had in a while, and was reluctant to end the experience quite so soon. Deciding that vigilante justice wasn't his cup of tea, he chose to stay and finish, even indulging in a lovely raspberry cheesecake tart with lemon and vanilla bean sauce for dessert, before heading for the concierge desk.

"I trust that your evening was satisfactory?" Francois smiled as the artist approached.

"As always, my good man," he slipped the concierge another fifty. "I am curious about something though..."

"Yes? What is it Mr. Kellerman?"

Kel took a gamble and hoped that his many years of generous tipping were about to pay off. He thought that he could trust the ultra-polite Parisian, and didn't want to even think about the consequences if Francois ratted him out.

"I noticed that Mr. Cramer seemed to leave in a hurry. I know the poor man must be grieving, and I was just hoping that everything was okay with him. I saw you give him a message and hoped it wasn't more bad news," the artist explained, hoping against hope that he hadn't overplayed his hand.

Francois stared at him blankly for so long that Kel began to wonder if the concierge had pushed a hidden button and was merely waiting for security to come and spirit him away. Finally, he took a breath, let it out slowly and spoke.

"We all...handle our grief in different ways, Mr. Kellerman," he said carefully, his expression revealing that there was more to the story.

"Indeed," Kel nodded, pursing his lips. "For instance...when I'm grieving, I like to spend time with special people in my life," he led the Frenchman.

"It seems that Mr. Cramer has a "special friend" with whom he likes to spend time...grieving, as well," Francois raised an eyebrow.

"I have to wonder if Mr. Cramer and I might have any mutual "special friends?" the tap dance continued, the muscles at the back of the artist's neck stiffening from tension.

"Perhaps. Is Miss Carolyn Latimer one of your special friends? Because I believe she is "consoling" Mr. Cramer as we speak. The night before that, it was Miss Marian Michago. Mr. Cramer seems to have no end of...special friends, Mr. Kellerman," the Frenchman revealed in a low voice.

"So it would seem," Kel agreed with a grim smile, handing him yet another fifty dollar bill. "It has been a great pleasure seeing you again, Francois," he shook hands and went to the front door just as the valet pulled his car up.

"The pleasure is mine, Mr. Kellerman. Come back soon," he bowed slightly.

Chapter 8

*S*pencer had been tasked with manning the front counter of *Cupcakes in Paradise* while Missy and Maggie discussed changes to the menu for the party with the catering manager. Never one to just sit and wait for a customer to walk in, the industrious and efficient Marine refilled the silverware containers, topped off the creams and sugars, wiped down every chair and table in the shop with a diluted bleach solution, arranged the plates, bowls and mugs behind the counter in a fashion that made them more accessible and easier to put away, and cleaned out any trash that he saw.

There was a brown paper shopping bag under the cash register that he pulled out, thinking it was trash, but when he looked inside, there was a well-worn brown teddy bear at the bottom. Closer examination of the stuffed animal revealed a split seam in the back. Spencer tucked the bear away inside the shopping bag and placed it in his backpack. He'd learned to sew when he was twelve, and being a man of action, he planned to take the bear to his place after he closed up shop. He'd repair the animal, then give it back to Missy to return to the rightful owner.

The afternoon passed quickly for the young veteran, with holiday shoppers coming in for a relaxing treat, and customers placing their holiday party orders. In no time at all, Spencer shouldered his backpack and headed for his apartment to do emergency surgery on someone's beloved bear. He fixed himself a snack, turned the TV on for company, and grabbed his sewing kit out of a drawer in the kitchen.

Finding the brown thread and a needle heavy enough to punch through the furry fabric, he pulled the bear out of the backpack, and noticed that there were tufts of stuffing coming out of the split seam in the bear's back. Tucking the stuffing back inside, his finger hit something that felt like hard plastic. Curious, he reached into the split with two fingers, wiggling them into the center of the bear and closing around a cylinder that was wedged inside. Carefully pulling his fingers out, he held, along with several puffs of fluffy white polyester, an amber plastic prescription pill bottle. He turned it around to read the label, and raised his eyebrows when he saw the name on it.

Spencer took all of the stuffing out of the bear to see if there were any other secrets hidden inside, but came up empty-handed. Setting the shell of the bear aside, he pulled his cell phone out of his pockets and dialed.

"Chas, there's something down here that you might want to take a look at," he said, when the detective answered the phone.

Chapter 9

"So, Cal Cramer is a bit of a scoundrel?" Missy asked, tearing a Coconut Dream cupcake in half so that she could bite it more easily.

"Apparently," Kel nodded with a grimace.

"Well, that would explain why he might want to kill his wife and his mistress," Echo made a wry face.

"It could explain that, yes."

"Did you find out who the two men sitting with Cal at the Club were?" Missy asked, swallowing a bite of cupcake and washing it down with coffee.

"I looked them up in the Club directory. One was Cal's lawyer, the other was his accountant."

"Hmm...that seems a little bit fishy. A man whose wife just died, having dinner with his lawyer and accountant," Missy's eyes narrowed suspiciously.

"Not necessarily," Echo chimed in practically. "They could have been going over Marcia's will or something."

"Or...they could have been discussing how to invest what I'm sure was a sizable insurance settlement," Kel pointed out.

"But Cal is already wealthy...surely he wouldn't have

killed his wife for the insurance policy. And he wouldn't benefit at all from killing his girlfriend, right?" Missy asked, thinking.

"Unless of course, she had threatened to expose him," the artist guessed.

"What do you mean?" Echo asked, watching the two of them go back and forth like a tennis match.

"Melany may have threatened to expose Cal's... habits, if he didn't leave his wife."

"But, Melany was already married, why would she ask him to leave his wife?"

"Perhaps so that the very wealthy father of her child could marry her and help her raise their daughter," Kel shrugged. "Who knows? It's all conjecture thus far."

Missy's eyes widened as realization struck.

"What?" Echo demanded, seeing her reaction. "What are you thinking?"

"Maybe one person didn't do all of the killing," she began slowly. "Maybe Melany killed Marcia to get her out of the picture, then Cal killed Melany so that she wouldn't reveal his secret...and of course, then he'd have to kill Garret, so that there'd be no witnesses..." she suggested.

"Hmm...I can't say that I could ever picture Melany Anderson even touching a gun, much less killing her best friend with one," Kel shook his head.

"Maybe Garret and Marcia conspired to kill Melany and Cal killed them for it," Echo supplied.

"I can't see Garret killing his wife. That would set him up for being a single parent, and to a child who might not even be his own. No, I can't see that happening," Kel shot the proposition down.

"So then, we're back to Cal killing all of them," Missy summed up. "We just need to figure out why."

"Maybe he wanted the kid," Echo guessed.

"Clearly you've never met Cal Cramer," Kel said dryly. "I'll be doing some checking around to see if I can figure out why the man who "had his cake and ate it too" would have a reason to slaughter three people, leaving a poor little girl orphaned." He stood to go, pushing in his chair and taking his plate and mug to the kitchen. Saying goodbye to the ladies, he headed out the door in search of the truth, no matter how horrible it might end up being.

"So, what happened with the party over at the inn?"

Echo asked, after he left. "Is it still on, or did they end up canceling?"

"It's still on, but on a slightly smaller scale, which means that we may have Cal Cramer right here in our midst," Missy replied, looking slightly worried.

"Sounds like Kel and I need to make an appearance at the party," Echo observed.

"My thoughts exactly."

The bell over the door jangled, and a thirty-something, somewhat bedraggled man came in. His hair looked like it hadn't been washed in a while, he had at least three days beard growth on his face, and his well-worn clothing hung loosely on his tall, thin frame. It was unusual to see a homeless person in this part of the Calgon beach community, but it happened from time to time. When they wandered in on occasion, Missy would give them a hot cup of coffee, a cupcake from the case, and a card for the shelter downtown. She often took leftover food from parties as well as day old baked goods to the shelter, and knew that that people who worked there were kind, genuine souls who would do everything that they could to help someone who was down and out.

"Good morning," she said cheerfully, hoping that the man was harmless.

"Hello," he replied softly, his eyes darting about nervously. "Are you Mrs. Beckett?"

Surprised that he knew her name, Missy nodded. "Yes, I am. How can I help you?"

"Well, I don't want to be a bother. Carla Mayhew sent me over here. I'm Brian Holman, Melany Anderson's brother. I was planning to go visit my niece today, over at the foster place, and Ms. Mayhew said that you might have her teddy bear. I figured since I was going over there, I might as well take it with me...save you the trip," he shrugged.

"Oh, how nice of you. Let me go get the bear. Carla dropped it off the other day," she said, rummaging under the front counter where she had left the bear. "Hmm...that's strange. It's not here. I know I left it under the counter," Missy stood perplexed, hands on hips.

"Maybe Chas took it over," Echo suggested.

"Chas?" Brian was confused.

"My husband. He's the detective working on your sister's case. I'm so sorry for your loss," Missy said, gazing at him with compassion.

"Oh. Well...uh, thanks for checking. I...uh...have to

go now. Thanks again," he said, seeming agitated and heading for the door.

"Hey, would you like a cup of coffee or a cupcake or anything? It's on me," Missy offered.

"No. I...have to...I just...no, thanks," he stammered, backing out the door.

Echo and Missy looked at each other, eyebrows raised.

"Poor guy, he looks like he's been through a lot," Echo observed.

"I know what it's like to lose a sister," Missy said, thinking of a painful time in her past. "It can really mess with your head," she bit her lip.

"You okay?" Echo asked, frowning with concern.

"Yeah, I'm fine," she replied, seeming to shake it off. "Ghosts of days gone by."

"Strange that he didn't want coffee or a cupcake. I thought that he was homeless," Echo changed the subject.

"Me too. Oh well, guess you can't judge a book by its cover."

Chapter 10

*D*etective Chas Beckett pulled up to the Cambridge Club and handed the keys to his non-descript beige police sedan to the uniformed valet, who looked at him curiously. He flashed his badge and the young man took care of the car without a word. Chas didn't appreciate meeting on someone else's turf and terms, but he didn't want Cal Cramer to get away with not being interviewed, so he agreed to meet the busy executive at the Cambridge. Having been raised the eldest son of a multi-billionaire, and inheriting a massive fortune upon his father's death, the detective wasn't the least bit intimidated by the venue, but was confident that that had been Cal's intention.

The concierge was expecting him, and led the detective to a quiet corner of the lounge.

"Mr. Cramer will be with you momentarily," the tuxedoed man with the profound French accent assured him.

Now Chas was even more irritated. He glanced at his watch and noted that Cal was late. The detective hadn't been born yesterday, and recognized a power play when he saw one. But, ultimately, the games didn't matter. Cal Cramer might insist on calling all the shots when it came to where and when, and might be trying to flex some muscle by making Chas wait, but if he was guilty of a heinous crime, he would still be treated like a common criminal. His obnoxious behavior would just make seeing him in prison orange all the more palatable.

"Pardon my tardiness, Detective," Cramer walked up briskly, pulling out a chair and seating himself, making sure that the knifelike creases in his trousers weren't compromised by the action. "I was unavoidably detained."

"By someone who wears a lovely shade of red, judging by the lipstick on your collar," Chas observed, unsmiling.

Cramer's eyes instantly became icy chips of grey flint. "Not that it's any of your business, but I was consoling a dear friend of my wife's," he said coldly. "Why exactly are we here?" the executive asked, flicking the cuff of his pinstriped sleeve back to glance at his watch. "My time is limited, so I'd like to get this over with as soon as possible."

"Nice watch," Chas observed, ignoring Cal's questions and demands. "Is it new?"

"I have no idea. I pull out my watch drawer and select the model that compliments my suit for the day. Why are we wasting time chatting about time pieces, exactly?" he demanded.

"Rolex, right?"

"You have a good eye, Detective, but really...will you please get to the point? I don't have time for games."

"Well then, perhaps you'll have time to explain to me why I found a receipt for a Rolex right outside the front door of a crime scene," the detective sat forward, raising an eyebrow in challenge.

"I have no idea," he shrugged. "Rolexes are a dime a dozen around here," the executive smirked. "Probably every third man in this club at any given time is wearing one. Just what precisely are you trying to imply, Beckett?"

"Where were you on the night that your wife was murdered, Mr. Cramer?"

"I was here. Lots of witnesses will be able to confirm that."

"When time did you leave the club?"

"I don't recall. I'd had a few drinks."

"Did you drive after having had those few drinks?" Chas challenged.

"I'm a law-abiding citizen, Detective. I wouldn't dream of such a thing," Cramer oozed sarcasm.

"I wonder if the security tapes from that date will back up your story."

"This is a private club, you don't have access to those tapes and you know it," Cal smirked.

"I can see how you would want that to be the case, but the fact of the matter is, I've already seen them," Chas informed him casually.

Cal Cramer tented his fingers in front of his lips and took a breath, studying the hard as nails lawman in front of him.

"I think we're done here, Detective Beckett. If you require any further information, you can talk with my attorney."

"Got something to hide, Cramer?"

"You can get up and walk out of this establishment right now, or I'll summon security and have you thrown out," the executive threatened. "Can I make myself any clearer than that, Beckett?"

"In time you will," Chas promised, unfazed.

The detective stood slowly and tossed his business card in front of the silently fuming man in front of him. "Call me if you think you'd like to amend your story."

Cramer snatched the card up from the table, viciously tore it to pieces and threw them on the floor.

$\mathcal{M}$issy sank gratefully into a warm bubble bath after a long day. She'd finally gotten all of her ducks in a row. The party for her guests was going to be much tamer and more intimate, with round tables and chairs set up in the ballroom. The DJ who had been originally scheduled was being replaced by an orchestral trio, to establish a mellower mood, and the good-hearted fellow had even agreed to return Steve Jeppson's deposit when he heard what had precipitated the change in plans. The menu had been adjusted from just hot hors d'oeuvres to appetizers and dinner with dessert, and Spencer would be tending the bar.

The decorating was done, all arrangements had been finalized and paid for in full, so now, she could actually breathe for a moment. Chas brought home Chinese take-out for dinner, and they'd eaten the savory food sitting on the couch in front of the TV. He'd gone to Spencer's basement apartment after receiving a text from the Marine, and Missy had poured herself a glass of crisp white wine, lit her vanilla scented candles and run her bath for a much-needed respite from the holiday frenzy.

She was thankful that Spencer had covered for her at the cupcake shop, the Marine had done every-thing perfectly, from taking orders, to cleaning, to closing. Tomorrow, she planned to go with Echo to shop for a holiday dress to wear to the party and Kel's gala – she was envisioning something sparkly, bright and dramatic, and was looking forward to girl time – but for now, it was time to relax and unwind.

Toffee, her beloved golden retriever, and Bitsy, Toffee's maltipoo canine sidekick, had wandered into the bathroom with her and were curled up in a corner near the vanity, enjoying the jazz playing on the docked iPod. Golden curls piled atop her head, Missy eased into the water up to her neck, sighing with pleasure. Her muscles relaxed and she closed her eyes. Time trickled by, and she might've fallen asleep if it hadn't been for the low growls coming from the dogs some time later, just as her water began to cool.

Missy opened her eyes and saw both dogs standing, hackles raised, looking toward the window. The master bathroom was on the second floor, so Missy had no idea as to what they could possibly see or hear, but she stepped out of the tub and slipped into her terrycloth robe to take a look. She peeked out of the blinds, seeing nothing. Staring into the darkness, unable to detect any movement or strange shadows, she attributed their response to an overreaction to normal night sounds, like the wind riffling through palm fronds and palmettos.

She was already in bed when Chas came in, about an hour or so after her bath.

"Everything okay?" she asked.

"Yup, just fine," her husband kissed her on both cheeks and then on the lips. "How was your bath? You smell great," he smiled appreciatively.

"Thanks. Lavender bath beads," Missy explained. "Hey, when you were walking to and from Spencer's apartment, did you see or hear anything...weird?"

Frowning, the detective shook his head. "No, but you've definitely captured my attention. Did something happen?"

"I don't know. Probably not," she yawned hugely and plumped her pillow up under her head. "Toffee and Bitsy were just staring out the window and growling. It was probably just the wind that had them spooked or something," she murmured, on the verge of sleep.

"Do you want me to go have a look at the grounds, just to ease your mind?" Chas offered.

"Nope, I'm fine," Missy assured him, unable to keep her eyes open any longer.

Chapter 12

"Mrs. Beckett, you need to come down to the shop as soon as possible," Spencer told Missy over the phone, early the next morning.

"Okay, I'm on my way," she said, slipping her feet into her soft, worn boat shoes and topping off the coffee in her to-go mug. "Are you okay?"

"I'm fine, ma'am."

"Good, I'll see you in a minute," she promised,

hanging up and shoving her phone into the back pocket of her jeans.

Spencer was waiting for her in front of the shop.

"I don't know how it happened, but when I got here to meet the delivery truck this morning, I found this," he said, opening the front door.

Missy gasped, tears springing to her eyes. Her shop had been ransacked. Shards of broken dishes littered the floor, trays of silverware had been dumped and sugar bowls emptied. Every bit of furniture was strewn about, and everything had been knocked off of the shelves behind the counter. The horrified owner shook her head in disbelief as she surveyed the mess.

"The kitchen is worse than this," Spencer said quietly, standing beside her.

"How can it be worse?" she asked, wrapping her arms around her midsection, feeling violated and scared.

Spencer moved toward the kitchen and Missy trailed after him, not wanting to see what had been done.

"It *is* worse," she whispered, bringing her hands to her mouth. Every ingredient had been spilled, poured out and scattered in the normally spotless stainless-steel kitchen, even chilled and frozen foods from the large walk-in refrigerator and freezer. Cartons of eggs had been tossed across the room, giant vats of butter had been scooped out and left to melt in lemon-yellow blobs on the countertop, and gallons of milk had been emptied into the sink. Bags containing dry ingredients had been slashed open, their contents spilling out onto the shelves and floor, even the peanut butter jars had been emptied, their contents smeared on the wall by the sinks.

"Why on earth would someone do this? It's senseless and cruel," Missy stared at the mess in disbelief.

"I thought at first that it might have been to cover up a robbery, but when I looked in your office, every drawer had been dumped, every cabinet emptied, but the safe was completely untouched. It doesn't look like anything at all was taken," Spencer informed her.

"Then why? Why would anyone do this?"

"Is there anyone who might want to hurt you?" the Marine asked, his jaw muscle flexing.

"No. Not her. Me," Chas spoke from behind them, standing in the doorway of the office. His eyes met Spencer's and a look passed between them that Missy couldn't fathom.

"You know who did this?" she asked, looking from one to the other.

"I have some leads to follow up on, but I have a pretty good idea. Don't touch anything, I'm going to have my guys come out and see what they can find," the detective instructed.

"Got something," Spencer said, kneeling down and pointing to an upended metal drawer.

"What is it?" Missy asked, not wanting to look.

"Blood," Chas said. "Let's get you out of here."

"How am I going to prepare the orders for my holiday customers?" she worried.

"I had the supply delivery stashed in the kitchen at

the inn when I saw this mess. Whatever you need that you don't have, I'll go to the wholesale store and get for you," Spencer assured her. "Echo and I can help with the baking, and Maggie can help us box things up. We can handle this and your customers will never know the difference."

"Thank you," Missy nodded, overwhelmed.

"Spencer, take my wife back to the inn so that you two can start planning for those orders. I'll take over here," Chas directed, reaching for his phone.

"Yes, sir," the Marine replied, leading Missy from the horrible mess that her sweet little shop had become.

On the way back to the inn, they cut through the parking lot, headed for the back door, and Missy pulled up short.

"Ma'am?" Spencer said, wondering what was wrong.

"Spence, does my trunk look like it's ajar?" she asked woodenly.

"Stay here, Mrs. Beckett. I'll check it out."

The Marine sidled up to the car slowly, and, using a stick that he picked up along the way, he pushed up on the trunk, not surprised in the least when it opened easily. The trunk was empty, but it too had been ransacked. The cover over the spare tire had been removed, and the carpet pulled away from every inch of the cargo space's interior.

Moving around to look in the windows, Spencer also found the driver's door ajar, the alarm disabled, and the contents of the glove compartment and center console strewn about.

"Spencer...what is going on around here?" Missy asked fearfully, standing several feet away from her car.

"This isn't random, ma'am," he replied grimly. "Someone is looking for something."

Chapter 13

"*B*ut what could you possibly have that would cause someone to tear your entire shop and your car apart?" Echo asked, adding flour to her mixing bowl in the inn's spacious kitchen.

"I have no idea. I'm still shaking just thinking about it," Missy replied with a shudder.

"Betsy warned me," Kel lamented, perched on a barstool, wearing a red and white striped apron.

"Who the heck is Betsy, and what did she warn you about?" Echo stopped stirring.

"Let's just say she's a "source." She warned me not to look too closely at Cal Cramer, because he's known to be ruthless."

"Surely, someone with as much money and influence as Cal Cramer wouldn't stoop to trashing my business and car," Missy was skeptical. "Particularly if it was just because you were snooping around."

"Don't you think that clever husband of yours has interviewed him by now?" Kel raised an eyebrow. "As the lone survivor in the group of philandering dolts, he'd be the first person that I'd talk to."

"So, he was trying to get back at Chas by scaring me?"

"What better way to hurt the husband than by tormenting the one who is most precious to him?" the artist shrugged.

"By that logic, someone else could've killed Marcia and Melany just to torture Cal," Echo pointed out.

Kel and Missy stared at her, as she went back to stirring her cupcake batter, and then looked at each other.

"I never even thought of that," Missy whispered.

"I'm on it," Kel said, hopping down from the stool and pulling off his apron.

"On what?" Echo was befuddled. "What did I miss?"

"It was your idea, silly!" Missy exclaimed. "All this

time we've been looking for proof that Cal killed everyone, even though it wouldn't really make sense for him to kill his wife and his mistress. What we really should have been looking for...maybe...was someone who held a grudge so big against Cal Cramer, that they were willing to kill just to hurt him. Think about it...someone murdered his wife *and* his girlfriend. If they were trying to get his attention and lash out, what better way to do it?"

"Right," Echo breathed, nodding slowly. "Wow, guess that makes me the clever one this time around, huh?" she teased.

"Maybe. But, now that we've figured out the why, we have to discover the who," Missy sighed. "And I still don't have any idea who trashed my shop, or why."

The two women worked well into the dinner hour, completing the cupcake orders and helping Spencer load them into the shuttle for delivery. Once the Marine was on his way to the first customer's location, Maggie made Echo and Missy sit down at the kitchen table while she made them a nice, hot dinner. Chas had called to say that he wouldn't be back until later, so they ate together quietly, both worn out by the stress-filled and busy day.

Kel took a gamble that he might just run into Rosemary Gambrioli, an administrative assistant in Cal Cramer's office, at one of her favorite lunch spots, Fusion Sushi, and his intuition paid off.

"Fancy meeting you here, pretty lady," he greeted his former lover with a kiss on the cheek.

The fit and stylish fifty-year-old was tastefully dressed in winter white slacks and a pink sweater set, with pearls adorning her ears and neck and her chestnut hair perfectly coiffed. Whenever the artist saw his former flame, he found himself wishing that the polished outer shell didn't house such a twisted core. When things were good with Rosemary, they were oh-so-good, but when things were bad...

"Well, look what the cat dragged in," she drawled pleasantly. "Join me?"

"I'd love a dose of your scintillating company while I consume my portion of prettified bait," Kel agreed, seating himself across from her.

"A simple yes would have sufficed," Rosemary rolled her eyes. "Some things never change."

"Indeed. You look as lovely as ever," he raised the water glass that the server had set down in front of him in a mock toast.

"Buttering me up already? You must need something," she observed shrewdly. "What is it this time, Phillip? What secrets of the universe are you harboring, and why on earth are you going to involve me in whatever scheme you're cooking up?"

"My dearest, is it so hard to believe that I'm simply delighted to see the one with whom I've spent so many pleasant hours of my life?" Kel raised his eyebrows, acting shocked.

"After you threw me out of your house and haven't so much as called or texted in nearly a year? Yeah, I have to say, I find this whole encounter a bit suspicious," she tapped her perfectly manicured nails on the table top. The server came and took their orders, saving the artist from having to answer right away.

Kel sighed. One of the things that had both pleased and annoyed him about Rosemary was that she had the uncanny ability to see right through him. When she had used that super power for the forces of good, life had been divine, but all too often she used her gift of insight to manipulate and destroy pieces of his soul, which was ultimately why he'd decided to keep his distance.

"Okay, you got me. I think there may be something sordid afoot, and I need some information from you," he decided to go with honesty in the interest of time. His friend could be in danger and he wanted the bad guy safely tucked away in a cell somewhere post-haste.

"Well, what do you know...he can be forthright sometimes," Rosemary observed cattily. "Just not in relationships unfortunately."

Kel bit back a reply as the server approached with their lunches. Tearing off the end of the paper, he opened his chopsticks and popped a piece of spicy dynamite roll into his mouth, chewing slowly to buy himself some time.

"Well, I can see that this was a misguided idea at

best," he sighed. "I'll finish my food and be on my way. I don't want to burden you with my presence for any longer than necessary," he attacked another slice of the roll.

"Oh, slow down and save the drama, Sally," she mocked lightly. "I suppose I can at least listen to whatever shenanigans you have in mind before rejecting you outright. It might even be entertaining," she blinked sweetly.

He considered leaving the rest of his sushi on the plate and just bolting, but time was of the essence in getting this mystery solved, which meant enduring Rosemary's barbs for just a bit longer. When he finally got down to asking the questions that he needed to ask, she was quite forthcoming. It frustrated him to no end that she answered all of his questions truthfully and without reservation, yet when he left, he had fewer answers than when he began.

Cal Cramer might be an arrogant sociopath, but Rosemary had seen every transaction that crossed his desk, and his behavior in business had done nothing to prompt a profound reaction like murder. According to his administrative assistant, who was definitely in the position to know, his clients were happy, as were his business partners and his associates. Cal Cramer made a whole lot of money, but apparently, he didn't make too many enemies in the process. Even rivals appreciated his negotiating skills and determination.

Chapter 14

*F*rustrated, the artist went back to his gallery. He'd be on his own today, since his gallery manager was helping Missy bake cupcakes. Kel used his code to get in the front door and immediately sensed that something was wrong, before he even flipped the light switch in the entry way. The sight that met his eyes caused him to sink to his knees in horror.

"No," he whispered, his voice hoarse with unshed tears. "No, this can't be real…"

In the clean, geometric spaces of the gallery which he'd worked so hard to make a reality, lay the broken bits and pieces of every sculpture that had been on display. Every painting and sketch that had adorned the walls was hacked into pieces and strewn on the floor. Years of creativity, hard work and grim determination had been destroyed in the time that it had taken to consume a sushi roll and drive across town.

Kel was utterly devastated. He dragged his fingertips through the dust of a pulverized sculpture, tears in his eyes. All of his hopes, his dreams, his livelihood...shattered.

"Why?" he whispered. He raised his dust covered hands in front of his face unable to take his gaze from the powdered destruction. Trembling he shouted at the top of his voice, "Whyyy???" that solitary word reverberating on the spotless white walls and polished steel beams.

Carla Mayhew was tired, sweaty and cranky and she

hadn't had a drink in several days, a fact that made her proud, but certainly not sweet-tempered. Her client today had been exceedingly annoying, and the movers that she'd hired for furniture placement were so entirely incompetent that she'd literally ended up kicking off her high heels and moving sofas, tables and chairs. The underarms of her designer blouse were dark with perspiration, her hair sprouted from her head in frizzy tendrils that would not be tamed, and any trace of makeup that she'd so artfully applied after her shower this morning, had melted from her face.

She hit the button to open her garage door, and of course, it refused to budge. That was the kind of day she'd been having. It seemed as though everyone and everything was doing its best to try to drive her to drink. Gritting her teeth, she parked in front of the door, got out, and entered her code into the electronic key pad. No response, of course.

She turned off the car, opened the back passenger door to grab her "tool" bag, in which she kept the implements of her trade – tape measure, paint chip samples, camera, laser level, and a basic tool kit, plus a mini-drill – tossing it over one shoulder and pulling a muscle in her neck. Wanting to scream with frustration, she reached into a small zipper pocket in her purse to grab her spare house key. Finally opening the front door, she dropped her bag in the foyer and gasped when she saw the state of her tastefully decorated home.

Everything was destroyed. Furniture was slashed and turned upside down, with the guts of chairs, sofas and pillows torn and strewn about. Vases and sculptures were broken to bits, and artwork was torn from the walls. Fearing that whoever had done the horrible deed might still be in the house, Carla ran outside without checking the other rooms, slamming the door behind her. She dialed 911 as she dove into her car and screeched the tires leaving her driveway.

Echo was bone-tired as she walked from the bus stop toward her little bungalow. She had just come within sight of the modest home in her up and coming neighborhood, when she saw her obnoxious neigh-bor, Steve, barreling toward her like a raging bull. Sighing inwardly, she braced herself for more of the awkward leering that oozed out of the man like toxic slime.

"Hi Steve," she greeted the man wearily, before she saw his wild-eyed state. "Oh, my...is something wrong?" she asked, a bit frightened about his seeming lack of mental stability.

"The little weasel outran me," he huffed, bending over and putting his hands on his knees, wheezing in an alarming manner.

"You were chasing someone, Steve? What's going on here?"

He raised a finger to indicate that he might recover in a minute, and concentrated on his breathing.

"Are you okay? Should I call an ambulance?" Echo worried.

"I heard some bangin' around, and stuff breakin' and I came out on my porch to have a look. I saw the little bugger comin' out the house, and I tried to chase him down," the neighbor huffed, sweat trickling down his puffy, reddened face in rivulets.

"A burglar? Was there someone in your house? Should I call the police?" she asked, alarmed.

Steve shook his head. "Not my house...your house," he wheezed.

The color drained from Echo's face. "There was someone in my house?" she whispered, terrified.

"Yeah," he made a choking sound, clutched his chest and fell to the ground, unconscious.

"Roberts, what exactly is going on here? My desk phone is lit up like a Christmas tree and I asked not to be disturbed," Detective Chas Beckett spoke sternly to the desk sergeant.

"Sorry, Detective. Thought you'd want to know that there's been a rash of vandalism and home invasion today," Roberts shrugged.

"Why would I want to know that?" Chas raised an eyebrow.

"Every victim of the vandalism is connected to you in some way, Beckett."

Spencer Bengal was replacing an outdoor faucet that was attached to the side of the pool house, when his cat, Moose, bounded over and began twining through his legs, purring. The Marine stood up straight, looking toward the inn, knowing that if Moose was out, it could only mean one thing... someone had tried to enter his apartment. He jogged to the back of the inn, every fiber of his being on high alert. He listened for any telltale sounds, and the banging that he expected was soon detected.

With his back to the rear wall of the inn, he crept closer to the corner and slipped around to the side of the building, where his apartment was located. As he inched closer, he could hear the muffled sound of the intruder trying to free himself. He lifted the pant leg of his khakis and pulled his knife from its sheath, never taking his eyes off of the apartment door. Now that he was closer, he could hear the frantic breaths being taken by the intruder as he tried to escape, he could smell the fear in his sweat.

Being trapped like an animal in a cage evoked a fear response so profound and so primitive in humans that it could actually prevent coherent thought. The more effectively a human being was restrained, the more panicked they became. Unless of course they had been trained to stifle and dismiss their fear response. Spencer's talent and training came back as easily as if he'd never made the return to civilian life. He moved without sound, he saw, heard and smelled without distraction, and he operated with perfect clarity and no fear.

Placing his knife between his teeth so that he would have the use of both hands, should he need them, the Marine moved like a panther toward its prey, dark and menacing. The unfortunate intruder who had dared to enter his realm, was about to experience a reality unlike anything he'd ever known.

here are you?" Chas asked urgently, when his wife picked up the phone.

"I'm with Maggie at the Inn, frosting cupcakes... why?" she asked, alarmed at her husband's tone.

"You need to lock every door and window and stay put. Have you seen Spencer?"

"Not since this afternoon. He was going to take care of some outdoor plumbing and maintenance today.

Why?" Missy was beginning to feel fear curling up and down her spine.

"See if you can get him to respond via phone or text. I've been trying to reach him and he's not answering."

"You don't think something happened to him, do you?"

"Definitely not. I don't think there's a situation that could come along that he wouldn't be able to handle," Chas replied confidently.

"Chas, what's going on?"

"I don't know yet, but I'm working on finding out, and when I do, we'll have the killer," he promised grimly.

"Be careful my darling," Missy pleaded, worried.

"You too, sweetie. Keep your phone close, I'll let you know what's happening as soon as I can."

After going through the house with Maggie and making certain that all of the doors and windows in the main inn were locked, Missy headed for the owner's wing. All of the guests were planning on staying in for the evening, and in the deepening twilight, the silence in Missy and Chas's part of the inn was deafening. Toffee and Bitsy followed her into the private quarters and waited patiently by her side while she locked the door separating the main inn from the owner's wing. She then went methodically through the downstairs checking every window and door, then repeated the process upstairs.

When the last latch had been securely fastened, she leaned against the wall next to the window, looking out at the deepening shadows before shutting the blinds. Something blinded her temporarily, and after she blinked rapidly to clear her vision, she saw a large shadow moving shakily on the grass outside the window, as if someone were standing there in the dark. A soft scream escaped her and she hit the floor, knowing that she was safe, but frightened anyway. The dogs whimpered and cuddled up to her while she lay on the floor, heart in her throat.

Spencer carefully extricated the fly from the spider's web, first taping his mouth shut with duct tape, to keep the powerless man from screaming for help...or mercy. His movements were smooth, effortless. He didn't have to think, his actions came naturally as he went about securing the man and rendering him harmless. The trap had done its job, detaining the prey until the predator could return and exact what he needed from the helpless creature contained in it. Whether the extraction would involve information, partial or total destruction depended largely upon the subject's pliability, and Spencer Bengal was terribly good at making his subjects...pliable.

Detective Chas Beckett looked at the list of addresses on his computer screen. Every one of them was tied to him in some way, and he couldn't help but wonder if it had been a result of his conversation with Cal Cramer. He hadn't taken the executive for a man who would exact that particular sort of revenge, but he'd often found that when dealing with ruthless people, nothing was out of bounds or off of the table. Grabbing his keys, he decided to head to Echo's bungalow first, simply because her house had been the only location at which the intruder had actually been seen.

Kel had wandered through the shattered remains of his once beautiful gallery and determined that every room and every piece had been destroyed. Even the file and desk drawers in the gallery office had been pulled out and dumped, the leather office chair shredded, with tufts of stuffing scattered about. The intruder had gotten in by disabling the security cameras in the rear of the building and cutting a hole in one of the windows. Feeling as though he literally no longer had anything to lose, the artist walked out the front door in a daze, leaving it unlocked.

Carla Mayhew was scared. Someone had violated her home, and she couldn't stop shivering. Sitting in her car outside an upscale bar called Tiki Town, she wrestled with the desire to go in and drink herself into oblivion. Tears rolling down her cheeks, she leaned her forehead on the steering wheel. She'd come so far. She was just getting to the point where she'd started feeling healthy again, like a fully functional human being. Her creativity was flowing, and her energy had increased. And now, the wind had been taken from her sails. She saw the long, dark hallway in front of her, and sat in the parking lot, debating whether or not to walk down it.

The decorator raised her head and saw a couple come out of the bar. They were a bit younger than she, and the woman was staggering a bit, being held up by her partner. She had no idea that part of her dress was tucked up into her waist band, and that the lacy edging of her undergarment was visible to whoever might be passing by.

Carla shook her head slowly back and forth. "No. Not me. Never again," she vowed, her eyes on the inebriated pair. She put her car into gear and drove two blocks down to a 24-hour restaurant that had an abundance of comfort food and a never-ending supply of decaf. She pulled into a spot, stepped out of her car, and walked toward the best decision of her new life.

In the company of a uniformed police officer, Echo trembled outside her home while his partner secured the house and searched for clues. Her neighbor Steve had been taken away by ambulance, looking grey, but still breathing, and she worried about him, despite the fact that their relationship thus far had been a bit contentious.

"Do you have any idea who might have broken in?"

the young patrol officer asked the distraught homeowner.

"No clue. I don't even have anything worth stealing. There are much nicer and bigger houses in this neighborhood if they were looking to find something of value."

Chas arrived and took over the questioning after a brief walk-through of the property.

"What's it like in there?" Echo asked fearfully, not sure if she actually wanted to know.

"Pretty torn up. Lots of destruction. That seems to be a theme recently," the detective grimaced.

"What do you mean?"

"First, Missy's shop, then, your house, Carla's house and Kel's gallery," Chas shook his head in disgust. "This wasn't a simple break-in and robbery. Something else is going on here."

All color drained from Echo's face. "The gallery?" she whispered. "What happened at the gallery? Is Kel okay?"

"As far as I know. I have guys on the scene out there now. Kel is nowhere to be found, but he called the incident in himself, so I'm assuming that he's okay."

"The gallery is his life," she murmured. "He worked so hard...well, at least he'll have his inventory. We can always clean up the building," Echo tried hard to be optimistic.

"From what I understand, every piece that was in the gallery was destroyed," Chas informed her quietly.

The heartbroken woman put her hands to her face and closed her eyes.

"Poor Kel. That poor, poor man...when will this madness end? What is going on Chas?" she opened her eyes and stared hard at the detective. "How do we stop this?"

"We find out who did it," was the determined reply. "Why don't you go sit in my car while we work on the scene? Once we're through here, you can pack an overnight bag and I'll take you to the inn."

Echo nodded numbly. "Is Missy okay? Has anything strange happened at the inn?" she worried.

"I spoke with Missy a little while ago and everything was fine. I have to believe that Spencer has things under control."

Chapter 16

Spencer stood in front of the wide-eyed and trembling man, muscular arms crossed casually over his chest.

"I'm going to remove the tape and you're going to talk to me. You're going to talk and not scream, because if you do, you'll lose the ability to ever scream again...even though you'll desperately want to," he explained calmly. "Are you clear as to my expectations?"

The man nodded vigorously.

"Do you understand that the consequences for misbehavior on your part will be...substantial?"

He nodded again, the whites of his eyes indicating the profundity of his panic. Spencer peeled the tape back slowly, taking a significant amount of skin from the unfortunate man's lips with it.

"Please," the raggedy man gasped when the tape was off.

"Stop," Spencer ordered. "Pleading will get you nowhere and only wastes my time. Your work is sloppy, so I know you're not a pro," he observed. "Your twitches, shakes and sketchy behavior rat you out. You're a junkie, and junkies don't have the proper motivation to do the sort of things that you've been up to, which means you're working for some-one. Who?" he demanded, his jaw set.

"I don't know what you're talking about, I just..." the

man's words were cut off as the Marine applied a certain type of pressure which rendered him unable to speak. He eased off and the man gasped.

"Okay, I'm sorry. I can't tell you who I'm working for. He'll kill me."

Spencer brought his face quite close to that of his subject. "If you don't give me some answers, and I mean now, death will be the least of your worries. Death will seem like sweet relief and a good option. Am I being fairly clear?"

The man mewled and jerked his head up and down. He resisted for a bit longer, but after exposure to just the surface of Spencer's many talents, he caved and revealed everything.

"Give me his name," the Marine directed, as his captive writhed in front of him, the smell of fear emanating from his pores so profoundly that it seemed to seep into the walls. When he complied, Spencer nodded, not surprised in the least.

"And what's your name?" he continued.

That answer was actually a surprise, but made a sick sort of sense. Spencer nodded slowly, twirling one of the tools of his trade between his fingers.

"Here's what's going to happen," he began, setting down the thin metal instrument.

"I'm going to call the nice detective who lives here, and he's going to arrest you, but before he does, you're going to tell him everything that you've told me, because if you don't, you and I are going to have another little visit. Don't make the mistake of believing that you'll be safe behind bars. Those kinds of limitations aren't even a challenge. I'll find you, and what you've experienced here today is a walk in the park compared to the things I'll share with you, got it?"

"Got it," the man whispered pitifully, broken.

"You're also going to explain to the nice detective why you were so desperately looking for this," he shoved the torn-apart remains of Emi Anderson's teddy bear in his face. It was the bedraggled man's undoing, and the tears that he had held at bay throughout the terrifying ordeal flowed freely.

"I'm sorry. I'm so sorry," he blubbered, his torn lips stinging from the salt in his tears.

"You should be," Spencer gave him a warning glance and pulled out his phone.

Chas answered his phone when he saw that it was

Spencer calling, knowing that the Marine wouldn't be on the line unless something of significance had happened.

"Beckett," the detective answered. "What have you got, Bengal?"

"I have the answer to just about every question that you have regarding the murders, the vandalism and the break-ins. He's sitting in my apartment – a bit tied up at the moment, but ready to give you his statement when you get here," Spencer replied.

"On my way," Chas was headed to his car when he hit the End button on his phone.

"We're going to the inn," he informed Echo when he slid into the sedan. "You can keep Missy company while I talk with Spencer."

"Did something happen?"

"Something did," the detective's response was vague, and Echo didn't ask anything more.

Chapter 17

*C*al Cramer had indulged one of his favorite mistresses, Melany Anderson, by allowing her to take home his prescription narcotics in the interest of taking the edge off of things and enabling her to cope with the grim realities of suburban life with her lackluster husband. Unbeknownst to him, his sweet little recreational girlfriend was selling the pills on the side. He should have put two and two together, when she offered him presents that he knew she couldn't afford.

Her skinflint husband made certain that the poor girl didn't have two dimes to rub together, yet she bought her multi-millionaire boyfriend a Rolex for his birthday. The fact that his preferred minx happened to be his wife's best friend, bothered him not in the least. He knew that Marcia had married him for money and status, and as long as she left him to his own devices and proclivities, it was cheaper to keep her rather than to divorce.

Chas Beckett knew that Melany Anderson had bought the Rolex, after tracing the receipt that had been found outside of her house back to the store where she'd purchased it. Security camera footage made it easy to identify the housewife, who had brought her lovely toddler Emi with her to the jewelry store to make the purchase. The detective had known that Cal had received the watch as a gift, before he ever set foot in the Club to speak with him, and found it interesting indeed that he hadn't admitted that simple fact.

Even odder was the fact that one of Melany's most regular customers was her brother Brian, who was addicted to the pills and couldn't function without them. His habit was to come over in the mornings, after Garret had gone to work, to purchase the pills from his sister and, if he was lucky, get a free meal as part of the deal. He felt guilty conducting such trans-actions in front of his niece, but rationalized that she was too young to know what was happening anyway.

The more addicted that Brian became, the worse his judgment got. When he wandered over to Garret and Melany's house on that fateful night, in a haze born of withdrawal and desperation, he had no idea what day or time it was, and was entirely thrown off to see other people in the house with Melany and Emi. He had demanded drugs the moment he was in the door, not taking the hint when Melany said that she didn't know what he was talking about. He was too far gone for subtlety, and became belligerent when his sister continued to deny his need.

Melany placed a hand on her brother's arm, pleading with her eyes, and he shoved her down on the floor, drawing a gun that he had in his pocket and waving it about with reckless abandon. Thank-fully, little Emi, hearing a bit of the shouting, had already climbed inside of one of the kitchen cabinets with her favorite bear, hands over her ears. Shots rang out, and the gun that had been borrowed by a small-time drug dealer, with whom Brian sometimes stayed in a gritty apartment two towns away, took the lives of his sister, her husband, and her best friend Marcia.

Brian Holman hadn't meant to hurt anyone, much less kill them, but there were two things he knew... he needed drugs, the faster the better, and he needed help. The kind of help that only big money could buy.

He knew that his sister had been regularly seeing Cal Cramer, she had confided to him over breakfast after selling him her boyfriend's pills. He also knew that she got her stash from the millionaire, and in his confused state, he believed that he could use that information as leverage.

"Where are the pills?" the executive demanded, when the filthy, crazed sibling of his girlfriend showed up at his estate and told him what had happened.

"I don't know," Brian whimpered. "I didn't have time to look. I had to get out of there. Someone could have heard the gunshots...I don't want to go to jail. I wouldn't be able to survive in jail."

"Find them," Cal ordered, speaking through his teeth. "You've been stupid enough to buy drugs from that liar, you're going to find that bottle and return it to me, or you're going to pay dearly. Your life is worth less than nothing to me. You will find that bottle and bring it back to me, or you will find yourself sucking in vast quantities of salt water somewhere between here and the Bahamas."

Brian nodded and begged for money and more pills so that he could think more clearly. Cramer tossed him a wad of bills and a couple of pills that he pulled from a silver case in his pants pocket. The junkie put the money absently in his pocket and threw the pills in his mouth, crunching them between his teeth.

"You should know where she kept them. If what she was doing was a secret that she kept from me, her husband, and everyone else, she had to have a hiding place. Where was it?"

"She kept the stash in the bear," the junkie mumbled, feeling the drug hit his system and finally relaxing a bit.

"What's that supposed to mean?" Cramer demanded, wondering if the useless sap was hallucinating.

"Emi's bear...she kept them in Emi's bear," Brian explained calmly.

"Then go get that bear," Cal ordered. "And bring me the bottle, or you're a dead man."

Chapter 18

"So, all of the destruction...the ruining of homes and businesses, was all caused by a murderous drug addict looking for a teddy bear?" Echo was incredulous.

Missy nodded. "Spencer was just trying to be helpful when he spotted the bear in the bag under the counter. He took it back to his place to sew up the tear in the back, and found the pill bottle with Cal Cramer's name on it. When he saw what had happened at the cupcake shop, he assumed that the two things were related, and told Chas of his suspicions. Brian Holman destroyed the shop at night, then the next morning he hit Carla's house as soon as she left for work. When he found nothing, he staked out the gallery, waiting for Kel to go to lunch, and did his search and destroy there. When that failed, he made his way to your house. How's your neighbor, by the way?"

"He's fine. It wasn't a heart attack, just a panic attack, so they calmed him down, told him to stop smoking and lose weight and sent him home with some tranquilizers."

"How did the murderer happen to end up at Spencer's?" Kel asked, seeming far more chipper than he had the last couple of days.

"By accident, actually. He thought it was a back door to the inn, which was his next target."

"So, he just walked in on Spencer?" Echo asked.

"I'm actually not quite certain as to how all of that

played out," Missy shrugged. "From what I understand, Brian opened up to Spencer, and by the time Chas got there, he made a full confession."

"Wow, so is Cal Cramer going to be held responsible for any of this?"

"Who knows? The DA is trying to decide whether to bother with charging him for unlawfully distributing narcotics. Brian is being charged with three counts of murder."

"Isn't it crazy how addiction can make someone so desperate that they'd do that to their own family?" Echo shook her head. "Speaking of desperation... you look like you might be feeling a bit better," she said to Kel, who smiled wryly.

"Indeed, I am, and I have a bit of a strange request for you both," the artist replied.

"We're all ears," Missy leaned forward.

"I would like the scraps and broken pieces of anything that was destroyed in Brian's frenzied search."

The two women looked at him curiously.

"Well, I guess that'll save me from having to rent a dumpster," Echo commented.

"Of course," Missy nodded. "You can have anything you'd like. Are you going to share with us why you might want it?"

"All in good time, dear ladies," he smiled at them affectionately. "All in good time."

Chapter 19

The caterer had set up in the staging area of the ballroom, the tables were aglow with candlelight, and the "snowy" sky that Carla, Missy and Spencer had painstakingly created, hung sparkling overhead. All of the guests were dressed in white, in keeping with the theme, and dinner service was about to begin. The foyer door opened, admitting a new guest, and Missy hurried over to greet the well-dressed man.

"Good evening and welcome to the Beach House. I'm Melissa, one of the owners," she introduced herself, impressed by the gentleman's white tuxedo and deliciously scented cologne.

"It's always a pleasure to meet such a beautiful lady," he kissed her hand, letting his gaze linger a bit too long on the graceful curves of her sequined white cocktail dress. "I'm Calvin Cramer."

Missy snatched her hand away like it was on fire.

"You have a lot of nerve coming here," she hissed, eyes flashing.

"I'm an invited guest," he chuckled. "I wouldn't have dreamed that a lovely little kitten like you would have claws. It's adorable really. Now, do be a dear and show me to the venue," he directed, oozing arrogance.

Just as Missy was about to give him a piece of her mind, the party's host, Steve Jeppson, wandered out into the foyer.

"Cal," he welcomed the treacherous snake with a handshake. "Good to see you out and about. It can't be easy for you right now. How are you coping?"

Raising an eyebrow and glancing ironically over at Missy, he replied. "As well as can be expected, I suppose." He followed Steve to the ballroom, leaving her steaming in the foyer.

Missy found Maggie in the staging area and pulled her aside.

"Darlin' can you oversee the party for me? I'm suddenly not feeling well," she explained all-too-truthfully. The very thought of Cal Cramer in her house turned her stomach. The philandering creep had paid the man who killed his wife and mistress, to trash her shop, Kel's gallery, Carla's house and the Inn. Who knows what might have happened if Spencer hadn't stepped in.

"Sure, no problem," Maggie agreed easily. "The caterer has this whole thing wonderfully under control – I would definitely use them again."

"That's great, thank you," Missy replied, distracted. "Have you seen Spence?"

"He's been lurking about in the doorway by the ball-room entrance," she chuckled. "You know how he is."

Missy nodded. "Yes, thankfully, I do."

She skirted around the main seating area, avoiding even glancing in Cal Cramer's direction, and found Spencer, resplendent in his all-white attire, standing like a sentry just outside the ballroom's entrance, as Maggie had said.

"Spencer..." she began.

"I saw him come in, Mrs. Beckett. I won't let him out of my sight," the Marine assured her, barely moving his lips. "The Detective is on his way."

"Oh? Is there something that I should know about?"

"Not that I'm aware of ma'am, just a precaution."

Missy clutched at the young veteran's arm, knowing how much he'd done to keep them all safe over the past several days.

"Thank you, Spence, for everything. You being here means a lot to us, truly," she smiled up at the Marine.

"No place I'd rather be, ma'am," he flashed his killer

dimples briefly, then looked past her to scan the room.

"When Chas arrives, would you let him know that I went home, please?"

"Of course. Have a good evening Mrs. Beckett."

"You too, Spencer."

Missy went back to the owner's wing and slipped out of her beautiful dress, pulling on comfy yoga pants and a well-worn t-shirt. It had been a rough week, and she didn't feel the slightest bit inclined to socialize with an arrogant executive who had wreaked havoc in her life. Chas came in about an hour later, bearing two platters loaded down with delicious food from the event.

"What are you up to?" she chuckled, relieving her husband of his burden.

"Celebrating," the detective grinned.

"Celebrating what?"

"The fact that I have the most beautiful wife in the whole world," he replied, kissing her. "And the fact that Cal Cramer just rode away from the party in the back of a police cruiser."

"He did? What happened?"

"The DA decided to prosecute him on the drug charges."

"Good riddance," Missy frowned.

"Well, the reality of the situation is that he'll probably do little to no time, but the fact that he's being prosecuted at all will send a message to those who think that they're above the law."

"At least that's something," she shrugged, removing the foil from one of the platters. "Let's eat, I'm starving."

"Maggie said you left the party because you weren't feeling well," Chas raised an eyebrow.

"Suddenly, somehow, I feel much better," she winked, and he swept her into his arms.

Chapter 20

"I can't believe that Kel still had the gala after everything that happened," Missy whispered to Echo as they milled about at the event.

The elegant redhead shrugged and sipped her champagne. "Maybe he needed a party to cheer him up."

The two of them surveyed the space that was now empty of art, but spotlessly clean. There was a lone large sculpture covered with a sheet awaiting reveal in the center of the room. In addition to having done clean-up after Brian Holman destroyed all of his precious art, Kel had painted the various geometric walls in shades of red, orange and gold, creating a vibrant warmth in the hard-lined space.

"What's under the cloth?" Missy whispered. "Do you know?"

Echo shook her head. "I have no idea. I begged him to tell me, or at least let me take a peek, but he wanted to surprise everyone. Oh yay, there's Carla," she couldn't keep the sarcasm from her voice when she spotted the decorator. Last time both of them had attended an event showcasing Kel's art, a very drunk Carla had pushed Echo into a sculpture, falling on top of her and destroying the piece.

"Ladies," Carla greeted them, giving Missy a kiss on the cheek and looking at Echo like a bug under a microscope. Clearly things were back to normal between the two of them, the brief respite from their snipe-fests apparently over.

"Please tell me that's punch in your cup," Echo commented nastily.

"Thus far, it's in the cup, but if you continue to speak, it may end up on that wretched dress of yours. Might be an improvement actually," she drawled.

"Okay, kittens, let's sheath the claws, shall we?" Missy put a hand on each of their arms. "Tonight is about Kel, and none of us is going to spoil his moment after what the poor man has been through," she reminded them sternly.

Carla opened her mouth to reply, but they were spared from her response by Kel tapping on his champagne glass on the second level of the gallery, where he held the tab that would raise the sheet covering his only piece of sculpture.

"Attention everyone. Attention," he called out,

waiting to speak until the room quieted down. "As most of you know, I've had a bit of a rough time lately, but I'm a firm believer that out of our most difficult times comes our greatest inspiration. When one has lost everything, one has to pull from the bottom of one's soul that which is good and charitable and filled with hope. From the ashes of despair, one must rise like a phoenix, so that the artistic voice is never silenced. Ladies and gentlemen, it is my honor and joy to present to you this evening....The Phoenix!"

The artist dramatically whipped the sheet from the sculpture, and a collective intake of breath stole the very air from the room. With the broken pieces and belongings that he'd gleaned from his former collection, Missy's shop and Carla and Echo's homes, he had crafted a glorious phoenix that rose majestically between walls of crimson, tangerine and umber.

Tears sprung to Missy and Echo's eyes, and even tough as nails Carla looked down for a moment, swallowing hard. Echo raised her glass, her eyes meeting those of her boss and friend.

"To new beginnings," she called out, unashamed of the tears that fell.

"To new beginnings," was the hearty reply from everyone in

the room.

Kel raised his glass to each of the ladies in turn, and drank to them all.

Chapter 21

The shop had been surprisingly easy to clean up when all of them pitched in, so the next week, Kel, Echo and Missy resumed their spots at the bistro table for morning coffee.

"There was a bidding war for The Phoenix," Kel announced, raising his coffee mug as a toast.

"That's understandable, it was breathtaking," Missy commented.

"I agree. I wish my house recovered as well as your business," Echo remarked glumly.

"Slow going?" Missy asked.

The redhead nodded. "There was a ton of remodeling to do before this whole mess, now it seems overwhelming. I just want to take a sledgehammer to the place and start over."

"Worked for me," Kel observed dryly.

"I'm sure Spencer wouldn't mind helping out," Missy suggested.

"I know, I already asked him," Echo grinned. "What's next on the agenda at the inn?"

"The Jeppson group checked out today, and thankfully, despite all of the weirdness, they left happy and booked another party for next year," she announced. "There's a newlywed couple coming in next week, and a whole bunch of cupcakes that need to be made and delivered locally."

"Wow, we're going to be hitting it hard all the way up until Christmas, aren't we?"

"That's the plan."

"Well, if you need a party conversation facilitator, do let me know. I'll try to make time in my busy schedule to help you out," Kel offered cheekily.

"You're always on the list," Missy assured the artist. She headed back to the kitchen to grab a tray. "Well, these are the last ones, enjoy," she directed, setting down the platter of vegan and regular Double Chocolate cupcakes with Peppermint Frosting.

"Delightful," Kel's eyes practically rolled back in his head. "And what little treats will you two be cooking up next week?"

"You'll just have to wait and see, but I'm thinking that you'll be pleased," Missy teased.

"That, my dear lady, is a foregone conclusion."

"Here's to good friends, good cupcakes, and rising like a phoenix," she beamed at her beautiful flame-haired friend and the ultimately talented artist, raising her mug. "I don't know what I'd do without you two."

"You'll never have to know," they replied in unison, clinking their mugs against hers.

A Note from Summer

By the time I wrote this book, nearly four years ago, I had been breathing, eating and dreaming Cozy Mysteries. I was still working at a pace of one book per week and had finally started to get the hang of it, or so I thought.

I love crime shows and have found that I can pull a ton of inspiration from them, specifically information about forensics and aspects of an investigation that tend to be more technical. I had obviously watched some serious crime shows before writing this particular book. When I went back to edit it, I was surprised at how...dark it was, and found myself having to tweak the content to make it more acceptable to a Cozy audience. It didn't get bad reviews the first time around, but I've gotten better at determining what is Cozy and what isn't since then (I hope), and thought I'd spare readers some of the details that were included in the first edition. The content and meaning is the same, the graphic nature is just a bit less profound and far more Cozy.

One of my struggles in writing Cozy, that haunts me to this day, is striking a balance between what is acceptable in the Cozy world and what is just too intense. Real life is messy and can be brutal, but when we read Cozy, we're looking for a bit of an escape from those sometimes harsh realities, so I've been making a conscious effort, for years now, to tone things down. My goal is to make the cleverness of the main character and the sweet atmosphere of the town and its people the focus of the story, with a dash of intrigue thrown in. I think I've done a bit better job of it lately than I did four years ago, and for that, I apologize. It's been a wonderful learning experience for me, and I always want to continue to learn and grow.

Thank you, dear readers, for taking this wild, wonderful journey through Cozy Mysteries with me! I couldn't do what I do without you, and I'm deeply thankful for your ongoing support.

Also by Summer Prescott

Frosted Love Series

Book 1: A Murder Moist Foul

Book 2: A Pinch of Murder

Book 3: Half Baked Murder

Book 4: A Mouthful of Murder

Book 5: Cupcakes and Murder

Book 6: Orange Marmalade Murder

Book 7: Buttercream Murder

Book 8: Teddy Bear Murder

Book 9: Honey Dripped Murder

Book 10: Devil's Food Murder

Book 11: Cereal Cupcake Murder

Book 12: Plain Vanilla Murder

Book 13: Strawberry Murder

Book 14: Raspberry Creme Murder

Book 15: Mango Madness Murder

Book 16: Chocolate Filled Murder

Book 17: Pumpkin Spice Murder

Book 18: Apple Cider Murder

Book 19: S'more Murder

Book 20: Chocolate Fudge Murder

Book 21: Gingerbread Murder

INNcredibly Sweet Series

Book 1: Irish Creme Killer

Book 2: Coconut Creme Killer

Book 3: Caramel Creme Killer

Book 4: Chai Cupcake Killer

Book 5: Streusel Creme Killer

Book 6: Peaches and Creme

Book 7: Marshmallow Creme Killer

Book 8: Boston Creme Killer

Book 9: Bourbon Creme Killer

Book 10: Spiced Latte Killer

Book 11: Toffee Apple Killer

Standalone Novels

A Match Made in Murder

Christmas Reunion Killer

Home for the Holidays

A Slippery Slope of Murder

A Twinkle of Murder

Thrillers

The Quiet Type

The Killing Girl

Blueberry Cupcake

Cupcakes

2 eggs at room temperature, separated

¼ tsp. cream of tartar

2 Tbsp (¼ stick) unsalted butter at room temperature

1 6 oz container blueberry yogurt

1 cup sugar

1/3 cup brown sugar

1/2 cup milk

1 tsp. baking powder

1 tsp. baking soda

2 cups cake flour **

1 cup frozen blueberries

Separate egg whites from the egg yolks.

Beat egg whites with ¼ tsp cream of tartar until soft peaks form.

Set aside.

Cream together butter and sugars until well combined, scraping bowl often.

It will look crumbly.

Beat in egg yolks, blueberry yogurt and milk.

Sift together baking soda, baking powder and cake flour.

Add dry mixture to the egg mixture. Combine well.

Fold in the egg whites.

Fold in the frozen blue berries.

Preheat oven to 350 degrees.

Pour batter to fill 2/3 of the cupcake liner.

Bake cupcakes for 15-17 minutes and check with a toothpick. If the batter does not stick to toothpick, then the cupcakes are done.

Makes 18-24 cupcakes.

**Can substitute for cake flour by sifting together:

Place 2 Tablespoons of cornstarch in bottom of 1 cup measuring cup, then fill cup with All-Purpose flour. Sift together and repeat.

Vanilla Buttercream frosting

2 Tbsp. (¼ stick) unsalted butter, at room temperature

2 cups powdered sugar

1 tsp pure vanilla extract

1/4 cup heavy whipping cream

2 Tbsp sour cream

Beat butter until fluffy.

Stir in sour cream and vanilla.

Alternating, beat in powdered sugar and heavy

whipping cream until desired consistency you desire.

Pipe onto cooled cupcakes.

Author's Note

I'd love to hear your thoughts on my books, the storylines, and anything else that you'd like to comment on—reader feedback is very important to me. My contact information, along with some other helpful links, is listed below. If you'd like to be on my list of "folks to contact" with updates, release and sales notifications, etc.... just shoot me an email and let me know. Thanks for reading!

Also...

... if you're looking for more great reads, I am proud to announce that Summer Prescott Books publishes several popular series by Cozy authors Gretchen Allen and Patti Benning, as well as Carolyn Q. Hunter, Blair Merrin, Susie Gayle and more!

Twitter: @summerprescott1

Blog and Book Catalog: http://summerprescottbooks.com

Email: summer.prescott.cozies@gmail.com

And...look up The Summer Prescott Fan Page and Summer Prescott Publishing Page on Facebook – let's be friends!

To download a free book, and sign up for our fun and exciting newsletter, which will give you opportunities to win prizes and swag, enter contests, and be the first to know about New Releases, click here: http://summerprescottbooks.com

48152296R00109

Made in the USA
Lexington, KY
14 August 2019